Huele el pan
que mi abuela hornea.

**Touch the bowls
my grandpa makes.**

Toca los tazones
que mi abuelo hace.

**Taste the fish
my uncle brings.**

Saborea el pescado
que mi tío trae.

**Hear the songs
my auntie sings.**

Oye las canciones
que mi tía canta.

See the dress
my mama sews.

Mira el vestido
que mi mamá cose.

**Smell the flowers
my papa grows.**

Huele las flores
que mi papá cultiva.

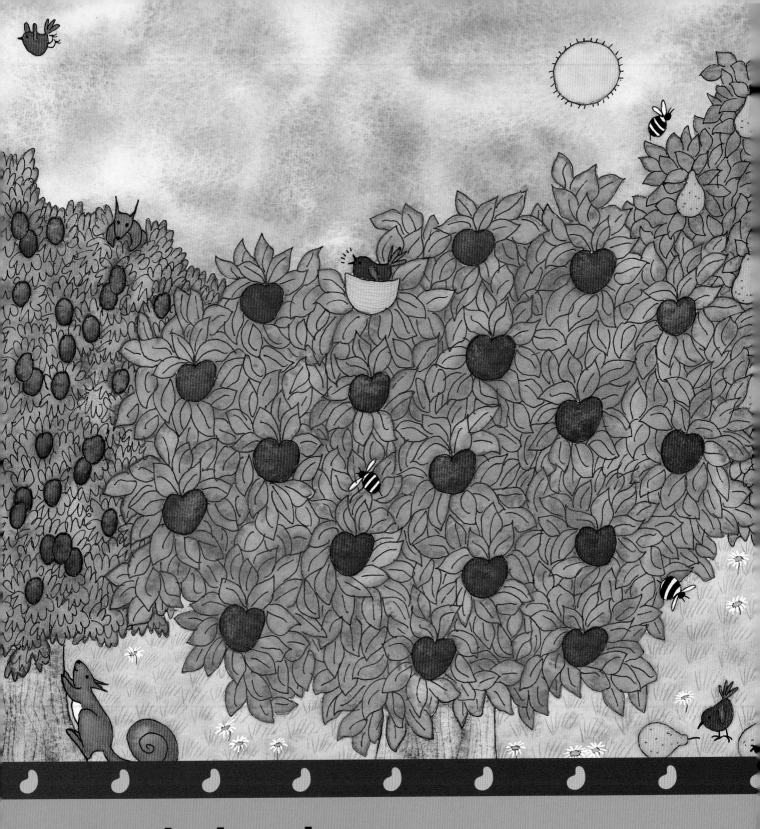

**Touch the plums
my sister picks.**

Toca las ciruelas
que mi hermana recoge.

**Taste the bowl
my brother licks.**

Saborea el tazón
que mi hermano lame.

Hear the drums
my cousins play.

Oye los tambores
que mis primos tocan.

See the feast for baby's birthday!

¡Mira el festín para
el cumpleaños de la bebé!

My Family Tree
Mi árbol genealógico

grandma
la abuela

papa
el papá

baby
la bebé

mama
la mamá

sister
la hermana

brother
el hermano

me
yo

grandpa
el abuelo

uncle
el tío

aunt
la tía

cousins
los primos

Vocabulary / Vocabulario

Hello. – Hola.
Good-bye. – Adiós.
Yes. – Sí.
No. – No.
Please? – ¿Por favor?
Thank you. – Gracias.
Pardon me. – Disculpe.
I'm sorry. – Lo siento.
How are you? – ¿Cómo está?
Fine, thank you. – Bien, gracias.

Barefoot Books   Barefoot Books
294 Banbury Road   2067 Massachusetts Ave
Oxford, OX2 7ED   Cambridge, MA 02140

Text copyright © 1999 by Stella Blackstone
Illustrations copyright © 1999 by Debbie Harter
The moral rights of Stella Blackstone and Debbie Harter have been asserted

First published in Great Britain by Barefoot Books, Ltd
and in the United States of America by Barefoot Books, Inc in 1999
This bilingual Spanish edition first published in 2012
All rights reserved

Graphic design by Tom Grzelinski, Bath and Louise Millar, London
Reproduction by Grafiscan, Verona
Printed in China on 100% acid-free paper
This book was typeset in Futura and Slappy
The illustrations were prepared in watercolor, pen and ink, and crayon

ISBN 978-1-84686-771-2

British Cataloguing-in-Publication Data:
a catalogue record for this book is available from the British Library

Library of Congress Cataloging-in-Publication Data
is available upon request

Translator: María A. Pérez

1 3 5 7 9 8 6 4 2